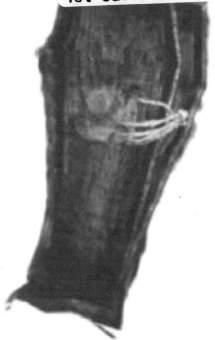

They're Coming For You
Scary Stories that Scream to be Read

Written & Illustrated
by
O. Penn-Coughin

You Come Too Publishing
Bend, Oregon

They're Coming For You *Scary Stories that Scream to be Read*
Published by You Come Too Publishing, Bend, Oregon.

Printed in the United States of America
First edition, 2008

Publisher's Cataloging-in-Publication

Penn-Coughin, O.
They're coming for you : scary stories that scream to
be read / written and illustrated by O. Penn-Coughin.
    p. cm.
SUMMARY: A collection of 27 original horror stories.
Some are seriously frightening, while others are
more humorous. Characters include wicked clowns, zombies
trying to get a little exercise, the ghost of a pioneer
woman looking for her lost child, ghost dogs, a phantom
soccer player, and others. Some of the stories have a
historical setting, such as the days of Lewis and Clark,
or the Oregon Trail.
    Audience: Ages 8-12.
    LCCN 2008925831
    ISBN-13: 978-0-9816836-0-7
    ISBN-10: 0-9816836-0-6
1. Children's stories, American. 2. Ghost stories. 3. Horror tales.
[1. Ghosts--Fiction. 2. Horror stories.]   I. Title.
PZ7.P384485The 2008
[Fic] QBI08-600140

For my old students
and the young ghost of my father

# Tombstone
# of Contents

Introduction
How to Read and Listen to a Scary Story

The stories in this book are meant to give you *da chicken skin* (as they say in Hawaiian, Dutch, Chinese, and Spanish) and make you laugh, think, shiver, and scream.

And while on the subject of screaming, here are a few tips for reading these stories aloud. Sometimes it's good to pause at the end of a story like it's over… and then let out an unexpected scream. Or you might want to scream near the beginning or the middle – just because. Other times you could really surprise your audience by having someone else do the yelling.

However, be forewarned: too much of a good thing is not always a good thing. Many listeners like the BIG SCREAM scary stories so much that they wait for the reader to yell at the end of every story. Of course, the more the reader screams the more the stories become predictable and lose their power. It's best to listen to each tale without too many expectations about how it will end. Just get lost in the story and enjoy it for what it has to offer. That way, when a scream does come, the effect will be that much stronger *and sweeter*.

These stories can be read in the quiet horror of your own mind or in a group. Several include read aloud instructions. Some of my personal favorites involve the use of accents. It's awesome fun to try to sound like a pirate, Southern grave robber, dead pioneer woman, French-Canadian voyageur, Irish soccer fan, or street corner thug. You don't have to use the accents, but they do add a nice touch. And don't be scared of sounding foolish. It's all part of storytelling.

Finally, remember to set the mood by turning down the lights and reading slowly and in a low voice, just above a whisper, until it's time to… SCREAM!

If you like this book, please ask your school to invite me for a visit. I'm just dying to meet you. In the meantime, visit me at CoughinBooks.com to find out about new books, contests, how to join the O. Penn-Coughin fan club, and other horribly good things.

O. Penn-Coughin

The Delicious Death of Jay Whitebread

Jay Whitebread was a writer of children's books. His specialty was scary stories. He was very popular with parents and teachers and that whole army of kids who said they liked scary stories just as long as they weren't *too* scary.

Jay Whitebread was their man.

He wrote them long and boring. It was like he had designed an amusement park full of roller coasters that just sat there. No one had nightmares and everyone went along for the ride.

On this one not-too-spooky night, Jay Whitebread was rewriting an old story about a woman who always wore a velvet ribbon around her neck. She never took it off. One night while the woman slept, her husband – who just couldn't stand it any longer – removed the ribbon. The story was supposed to end with the woman's head coming off and rolling onto the floor.

But Jay Whitebread thought that was much too violent. What would teachers say? What would parents do when their children woke up crying in the middle of the night? No, no, no. The head coming off just wouldn't do. So he changed the ending.

Jay Whitebread kept the woman's head **attached**. When the husband took off the velvet ribbon, all that happened was the wife waking up and saying, "Boo."

No nightmares there. A few more stories like that and Jay Whitebread would soon have another soft batch ready to send off to his publisher.

Inside his big mansion on the hill, Jay Whitebread rewarded himself with a little cup of vanilla ice cream and sat in his big leather chair in front of one of his five fireplaces, looking very pleased with himself.

Suddenly there was crazy laughter coming from the chimney and a pound-pound-pounding as if something was making its way down toward the fireplace. Standing now, Jay Whitebread dropped his little cup of vanilla ice cream when he saw what it was.

Out of the fireplace and onto the floor rolled the head of the woman from Jay Whitebread's story.

"You don't scare nobody, Mr. Writer!" it cackled, rising off the ground. "Maybe you should write romance novels!"

attached: connected.

The head floated closer and closer to Jay Whitebread's terrified face. From just a few inches away, it looked into his eyes and whispered, "Hey, you're kinda cute."

The head then closed its eyes, opened its mouth, and kissed Jay Whitebread on the lips.

Jay Whitebread turned as white as his vanilla ice cream and dropped dead. From outside the mansion, **hideous** cackling – and typing – could be heard long into the night.

hideous: very ugly.

The Clown
from Down Under

Elmer Rodríguez was one hard, little *hombre*. He never smiled. Never laughed. Always looking like his dog had just died – and so what if it had, what business was it of yours? I mean little dude was harder than getting up early on Sunday morning.

Elmer wasn't afraid of the teacher or the principal or those crazy *cholos* with the prison tattoos he had to pass every day on his way home. He wasn't even scared of getting beat up by the sixth graders.

There was only one thing the little eight-year-old was afraid of. And that thing came around once a year, every year.

For some reason, Elmer Rodríguez was scared lily white of clowns.

Sure, a lot of kids are scared of clowns. Nothing special in that. But Elmer was different. Clowns swallowed all the oxygen in a room and drained

hombre: *man* in Spanish.
cholos: a word with many meanings that here means *gangsters*.

his heart of all its blood. He was so terrified that his family had to stay away from the most popular fast-food joints because of the clowns.

In kindergarten he had even fainted when a clown came out to the school during the yearly fire safety assembly. All the clown had done was smile.

But that's all it took: one look at that ear-to-ear, painted-on smile left Elmer's lungs sucking for air and the room spinning.

It was the same time the following year – although Elmer hadn't learned how calendars worked yet – when the clown reappeared. The little boy took deep breaths. One after another.

The children laughed nervously and the teachers laughed through their bottom teeth the way adults do when something's not really **chistoso**. The laughter echoed through the school as the clown's smile cut into Elmer's soul like a rusty razor.

"*El payaso, no.* Not the clown," Elmer whispered over and over again, squeezing his eyes so tight that fat tears spilled down his bloodless cheeks. "*El payaso, no.*"

Speaking of fat, that clown was one *nacho grande*. And he wasn't even a real clown. He was just a fireman dressed up as a clown. Not that anyone would feel safe in case of a fire with this **panzón** around. Except for the donuts, maybe.

---

chistoso: *funny* in Spanish.
panzón: someone with a large belly (Spanish).

At the next assembly, when he was in the second grade, Elmer could have sworn that the clown looked right at him and mouthed, *"Hola, amigo."*

Elmer could see the clown's crooked yellow teeth smiling at him as its eyes danced like skeletons on *El dia de los muertos*. Those eyes were alive with evil and looking right at Elmer, burning a hole inside him that would always **smolder**.

As the years went by, Elmer wondered why the fire department would use a clown. What did clowns have to do with safety or fires or anything anyway? What did clowns have to do with anything except fear and evil and scaring poor little kids out of their minds?

When he was in the third grade, Elmer finally made up his mind that he would put an end to it. He stopped at a church before school to ask for help and forgiveness for what he was about to do.

As he got to school, Elmer saw the big red fire truck parked outside, and he knew that this was the day. His calendar skills had improved. When the clown started talking during the assembly, Elmer looked down and played nervously with his backpack.

Suddenly Elmer stood up and shouted *"No más, payaso!* No more!"

He then pulled something out of the backpack. Holding his breath, Elmer **hurled** a holy water-filled balloon at the clown and scored a direct hit on the thing's face. SPLASH!

smolder: to burn with little smoke or flame.
hurled: threw.

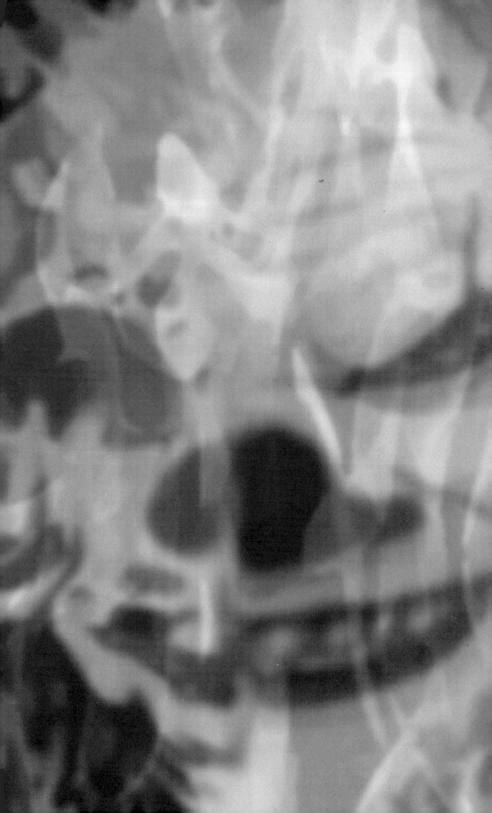

The principal looked at Elmer's teacher like someone had cut a real nasty one and the teacher reached over and grabbed Elmer hard by the wrist.

"What in…!" the teacher yelled but then stopped when she heard a loud gasp coming from the crowd.

In front of that entire gym full of kids, the clown burst into flames. The other firefighters emptied their extinguishers, but the flames just kept growing until the smell of burning clown filled the air. The make-up, the red plastic hair and red rubber nose, the big floppy shoes, the sweaty, smelly costume, and the thing's flesh all started to blur together.

The clown laughed at first but seemed to lose its sense of humor after the smile melted off its face.

"*Orale, pues.* All righty then. I'll be waiting for you down there, my little **vato**," it said in a low, threatening voice. "*Te espero, Elmer, eh? Te espero…*"

And then it was gone. A smoking, black stain on the gym floor was all that remained.

No one – including Elmer – was sure what had happened. The only thing Elmer knew was that he never wanted to see that clown again. He promised himself that from then on he would be good. Very, very good. *Muy, muy bueno.*

---

vato: slang for *man, dude, pal,* or *brother.*

You Come Too

"**S**tupid, stupid, stupid, stupid, stupid, stupid, stupid, stupid, stupid smelly ol' sub," Megan mumbled as she watched the other kids play outside.

Megan hated old, mean Mrs. Crankshaft because she was old and because she was mean. But mostly she hated her because she was smelly.

There were always bad things to smell at school: the lunch lady's awful offerings, the **stench** of those sweaty boys after recess, the kid whose underwear died last Tuesday without anyone bothering to bury it. The list went on and on.

But Mrs. Crankshaft took the cake when it came to bad smells. She took the cake and spread some nasty frosting all over it. Woo-wee!

That being the case, Megan thought it would be appropriate to make farting noises when the old woman walked by. She put the back part of her

stench: a strong, bad smell; stink.

hand to her mouth and let one fly. A few of the kids giggled.

However, it seemed Mrs. Crankshaft still had some life in her because she spun around quickly, squinted right at Megan, and whispered, "You just won an all-expenses-paid trip to recess in here with me."

So Megan spent recess looking out the window and mumbling under her breath.

"Stupid, stupid, stupid, stupid, stupid, stupid, stupid, stupid, stupid smelly ol' sub," she said to herself over and over again. But the last time she said it, Mrs. Crankshaft interrupted her.

"What did you say, girl?"

Megan turned around to tell some lie but stopped. Mrs. Crankshaft was staring at her with small, terrible eyes. Then the eyes got as big as golf balls. And then they were gone. Suddenly Mrs. Crankshaft **keeled over** onto the desk face first.

An ambulance came to take the old woman away, followed by every counselor in a 50-mile **radius**, and then the kids were sent home early.

"Are you all right, Megan?" her mom asked later.

"Yeah, I'm fine," she said.

That night Megan woke up to the sound of the floor creaking. In the darkness of the bedroom, she could see her mom standing in the doorway.

keeled over: fell.
radius: a circular area around a central point.

"Mom, I told you I'm fine," she said. "I don't care about Mrs. Crankshaft. I just want to sleep."

Megan's mom didn't answer.

Then, suddenly, the most horrible smell filled the room. It was that nasty frosting smell.

"Mom?" Megan said in a shaky voice. The smell just grew stronger, and then the figure began to move towards the bed.

"I heard what you said, guuurl!" A muddy, dark voice gurgled. "Call for your mommy if you think it'll help!"

Megan tried to scream but **gagged** on the smell and the fear.

The next morning an ambulance came and took Megan away. She would be spending recess with the sub again. Mrs. Crankshaft had saved her a place right next to her at the **morgue**.

gagged: choked.
morgue: a building (or room) where dead bodies are kept before burial.

Yo Mama's Right Here

The figure rose out of the water. The wet, black dress pressed in on her bony body. The tattered, black bonnet surrounded what had once been a face. Rotting, gray flesh with teeth and bone showing through. Empty, dark holes where the eyes used to be. Her hands reached out blindly for her dead child.

"Baby, come to meeeeee..." she moaned. "Yo mama's right heeeeeere."

With a scream, Jacob Brown woke up from his nightmare.

"Jacob, what's wrong?" his wife Mary asked.

"Bad dream is all," Jacob said, wiping the sweat off his face. "Get back to sleep now."

Tomorrow they would be crossing the Green River. Jacob always had trouble sleeping before crossings. To get an early start in the morning, the wagon train had camped near the river. Jacob could hear the sound of the dark water that was waiting for them.

"I would sooner rastle a bear than tangle with them waters," he thought.

But Jacob knew that if the family was going to get to the green farmlands of Oregon, they were going to have to cross this river. They had crossed others, and there would be more ahead.

He got up, pulled his boots on, and walked down to the river. Dawn still felt hours away. The moon did little to brighten the water or Jacob's troubled mind. After a while he walked back to the wagons.

In the morning a tired Jacob hitched the oxen to the wagon and smiled when he saw his three young children running around. Things were always better in the morning.

"Git on up here, you rascals," he told them. "It's time to go."

In the distance, dark clouds colored the sky. But overhead it was blue as the first wagons began to cross the river.

One behind the other, the heavy wagons moved slowly through the water, each making it safely to the other side. Finally it was their turn.

"Yaw!" Jacob shouted to the oxen. "Do work!"

By now the sky above had turned much darker and the water had begun to rise. The river was moving faster than when the first wagons crossed.

At first Jacob thought it was just his tired mind playing tricks on him. He could barely hear it above the noise of the rushing water.

"Baby, come to meeeeee…" it moaned softly. "Yo mama's right heeeeeere."

Jacob swallowed hard and continued to drive the team. The animals did their best, but to Jacob it felt like giant snails were pulling the wagon. The force of the water made it harder and harder to keep on course. It started to rain.

And then Jacob heard it again. She was closer and louder now, and Jacob had no doubt she was real.

"Baby, come to meeeeee…" she called again. "Yo mama's right heeeeeere."

Through chattering teeth, Jacob urged the team forward.

"Y-y-y-yaw!" he ordered in a shaky voice. "G-g-g-git going!"

The minutes seemed like hours, but through the now-pouring rain Jacob could see the shore ahead getting closer. He almost smiled at the thought that they would make it.

And then it happened. It happened just like in his dream.

Something rose out of the water right in front of the oxen. The wet, black dress pressed in on her bony body. The tattered, black bonnet surrounded what had once been a face. Rotting, gray flesh with teeth and bone showing through. Empty, dark holes where the eyes used to be. Hands reaching out blindly in front of her.

"Baby, come to meeeeee..." she moaned loudly. "Yo mama's right heeeeeere."

Suddenly, as Jacob screamed, the wagon hit a **submerged** boulder and rose in the air. Then, as Mary and the children screamed, the wagon tipped over. Jacob fell into the water and was carried downriver.

The last thing he saw before disappearing forever under the cold, black water was the woman floating above the wagon.

"Baby, come to meeeeee. Yo mama's ri..."

[Now quickly shout: AHHHHHH!]

Crossing rivers along the Oregon Trail was dangerous. Hundreds of pioneers drowned trying to cross the Kansas, North Platte, and Columbia Rivers – among others. In 1850 alone, 37 people drowned attempting to cross the Green River in Wyoming.

submerged: under the surface of the water.

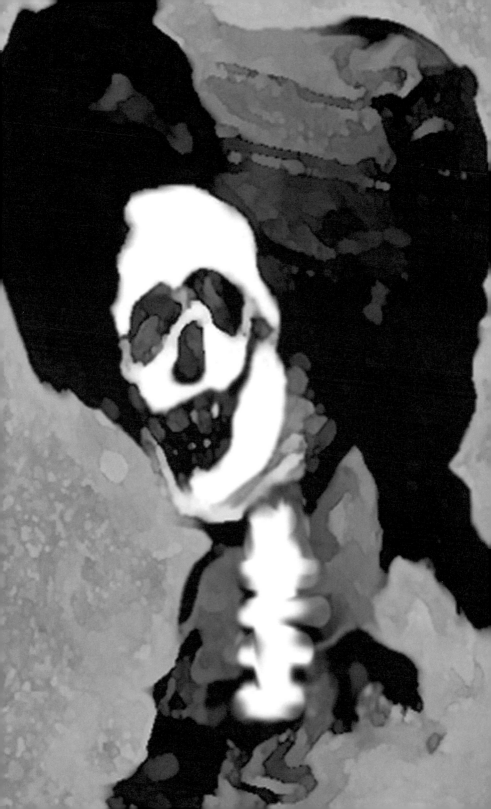

Little Plastic Guitar

Steve Reynolds had been resting in peace for more than 30 years now.

He had long ago given up on the dream of making it into the Rock and Roll Hall of Fame. He knew his songs were not classics. He had just done the best he could. And he had some fun along the way. Sure, like any other ghost he had some regrets. Mostly he wished he had not been driving so fast that night – that *last* night.

"But what's done is done, son," he told himself.

Lately, though, Steve had been doing a lot of tossing and turning in his grave. Back in the other world, one of Steve's songs had been included in the latest version of the *Little Plastic Guitar Superstar* video game.

At first Steve was mildly excited by the news. But then kids all over the other world started disrespecting his song.

"That song smells worse than a room full of angry bleu cheese farts," French children moaned.

"Nastier than your hairy uncle's armpits," the youngsters of Uruguay groaned.

"Total Godzilla poop," Japanese kids intoned.

Steve did his best not to lose sleep over it. But the little stinkers were relentless. Eventually, Steve got pretty **livid**. Then Steve got extra livid.

He knew he didn't have enough pull to put a complete stop to his **misery**. But a friend of a friend of a friend had done a favor for a man who could arrange it so that Steve could teach one little kid a lesson he would not soon forget.

Steve waited for the next insult to come his way. As it turned out, he didn't have to wait too long...

"Don't eat all the candy at once," Dickie's mom shouted.

"I won't," Dickie shouted back with his pie hole full of candy as he fingered the little plastic guitar.

"Not this song again," Dickie groaned. "This song is pure *caca*."

Not long after beating the game on normal level, Dickie fell asleep. His numb fingers were still twitching as the drool ran down his chocolate-smeared face. And then he had the most terrible nightmare.

---

livid: very angry: pale, white, or not having color.
misery: great suffering and sadness.

Dickie found himself in the game as part of the crowd. The band was playing the song – *that song* – and everyone, including Dickie, was loving it. He was like a puppet being controlled by someone else. Hard as he tried, he couldn't keep from pumping his fist into the air and shouting "YEAH! YEAH! YEAH!" over and over and over again.

It was hard to judge how much time had gone by, but it felt like hours.

"Wake up, wake up," Dickie whimpered as he slumped in his chair. "Make it stop. Just make it stop."

But Dickie couldn't wake up. And he couldn't make it stop. He was trapped. Trapped inside the game. Trapped inside that song. Trapped inside his little, screaming mind.

Cozy in his grave, Steve Reynolds was smiling. The little punk seemed to be having such an awful time that Steve figured there was no hurry in ending the nightmare anytime soon.

"Be cool, my man," he yawned. "Keep a rockin'."

He stretched his ghostly limbs and, for the first time since the game hit the stores, Steve slept like a baby.

Run for Your Life

Sarah hated her job at the mall. That was one reason she liked the track so much. By the time she finished a run, Sarah had usually forgotten about her idiot boss and all those annoying customers.

"The customer is always right," her boss would repeat. All Sarah knew was that sometimes they gave her a pain in the neck that wasn't exactly in her neck.

So every day after work, Sarah changed into her running clothes and shoes and drove over to the high school track near her home.

Another thing that was cool about the track was that few people used it. It was great to be outside and away from the crowds of the mall. But today was different.

Sarah was surprised to see more than 20 people going around in circles in the growing **twilight**. She was there a little later than usual because she had worked some extra hours.

twilight: the time between sunset and night.

"I guess it's more popular at this time," thought Sarah as she began warming up.

After a few laps, Sarah felt a sharp pain in her stomach. It was normal to have a few aches and pains at the beginning of a run. They usually just went away after a while. But this pain was getting worse. Then a terrible, burning burp came up Sarah's throat.

"That spaghetti sauce is trying to kill me," she said out loud, remembering what she had for lunch.

Sarah slowed down and began walking. For the first time since she arrived, she began looking closely at the people going around the track. They were all walking slowly, and they were all dressed in church clothes.

"What a bunch of freaks," Sarah thought.

She began to run again, but it was no use. The pain wouldn't let her. Sarah was now moving as slowly as the others.

Soon an old man in a brown suit started walking next to her. Sarah noticed that his face was very pale. But there was something strangely familiar about it.

"Saraaaaah," he said. "I have something to tell yooooouuu…"

Sarah stopped and began to ask him how he knew her name, but then as the old man turned to face her she saw that the other half of his face was completely eaten away.

Screaming, Sarah started running.

Forgetting about the pain, she ran as fast as she could. She ran to the parking lot. But her car wasn't there.

So she kept running. She ran and ran and ran. She finally looked over her shoulder, hoping that the old man wasn't somehow chasing her. There was no one there.

Sarah began to slow down, and then she saw her car up ahead in the middle of the street surrounded by a group of people. Suddenly she remembered who the old man's horrible face belonged to.

"Grandpa," she gasped. "But… he's been dead for 10 years."

The pain in her stomach came back stronger than ever as Sarah wobbled down the street.

She seemed to float past the crowd surrounding her car.

As she looked in through the cracked glass, Sarah saw herself. Her lifeless body was crushed under the steering wheel. Her eyes were open but saw nothing. And there was a dark, growing stain over her stomach that wasn't just spaghetti sauce.

Shot in the Gas Station

Chuck sat on the gas station toilet near the Montana-North Dakota border. He hated using these stinky public bathrooms as much as he hated using the ones at his school back in Oregon. But since his family was driving to visit his grandparents in Minnesota, Chuck didn't really have much choice.

So there he sat on the silly tissue-paper seat cover, trying to hold his breath and make some sense of the **primitive** poetry on the stall walls at the same time.

"Here I sit broken hearted, paid a quarter and only..."

Suddenly Chuck felt a terrible pain cut through his left butt cheek. Water squirted out of his eyes and a voice he didn't recognize exploded from his throat. "Blast you, Cruzatte, you have shot me! You have SHOT ME!"

Chuck woke up on the cold, dirty tile floor, his mind separated from any sense of time or place. He

primitive: simple, basic, crude.

thought he heard the sounds of a fiddle playing in the distance.

After a while Chuck reached down with his hand to check for damages, afraid of what he'd find. There was nothing there. And the pain was gone like the whole thing had never happened. Chuck got up slowly and shakily stumbled over to the sink. He washed his hands and wiped his tear-stained face. When he looked up, there in the mirror looking back at him was a bearded man with a patch over one eye wearing clothes made of animal fur. He smiled **sheepishly** through dirty teeth, a twinkle in his eye. And then he was gone.

"That was fast," his dad said **sarcastically** when Chuck finally made it back to the car. "You open up a bakery in there?"

A few miles down the road, Chuck's dad stopped the car at the historical display next to the highway.

To his astonishment, Chuck learned that the gas station had been built near the site where something **astounding** had happened 200 years earlier. It was close to the very spot where Pierre Cruzatte, the Lewis and Clark Expedition's one-eyed fiddle player, had accidentally shot Meriwether Lewis in the left buttock. It said that Lewis made a full recovery.

sheepishly: showing or feeling embarrassment.
sarcastically: making fun of someone or something.
astounding: surprising.

"All's well that ENDS well, eh, Chuck?" his father joked as his mom and little sister giggled. Pale as a ghost, Chuck felt his pants grow wet.

The historical aspects of this story are true. Lewis and Private Cruzatte were elk hunting at the time. At first Lewis thought Cruzatte – whose one good eye was not all that good – had shot him. Then he thought it must be Indians. Later Cruzatte denied having shot the captain. But Lewis found the bullet in his pants. It was the same type as Cruzatte had in his rifle.

One more thing: Since Lewis was the group's medic, he had to patch his painful wound himself. The man who helped him off with his pants was named Gass – Sergeant Patrick Gass.

Into the Woods

For years her dad would look out the kitchen window into the dark forest that was just past their backyard and say the same thing.

"Never, ever, ever go out into those woods alone." He snapped his head around toward Amy and stared at her with those black eyes. "Do you hear me? *Never*."

When she promised that she would never go there, he turned back to the window, lost in thought.

Most years Amy had never even thought about the woods. When she was younger she liked to jump on the trampoline and roller skate down their long driveway. When she was nine she liked to shoot hoops with her friends and go to sleepovers.

But now Amy was 11. She was 11 and she liked to think about things and sometimes be by herself. She really loved to draw and spent her weekends sketching. She was especially good at drawing flowers and trees and couldn't help thinking about all those giant trees in the woods.

One Saturday in April, her dad left Amy alone because he had to visit a sick friend who lived far away. He said he wouldn't be back until late and was gone when she woke up. After lunch she walked to the kitchen window and stared out.

"I'm not afraid of those woods," she said. Soon Amy had her art supplies and stood at the edge of the backyard, looking into the shady forest.

The deeper she went into the woods, the more beautiful the trees became. Eventually, Amy found a large boulder to sit on and started drawing. Time went by fast. Five or six pictures later, she glanced up and noticed the sun had grown hazy and soft and had fallen down low, peeking through only a few trees.

Although her dad wouldn't be back for a few hours, it was time for her to start back home. She packed up her pencils and jumped down from the rock.

As Amy walked through the forest, nothing looked familiar. The trees grew darker, becoming large **silhouettes** that surrounded her path. She started to worry. Everything looked the same and it felt like she was going in circles. Her mouth dried up and she was getting cold. She started to cry.

Suddenly a little boy came out from behind a tree. He was wearing muddy jeans and a large, dirty

silhouettes: the dark outlines of people or things.

T-shirt. His pale face was the only brightness in the entire woods.

"Why are you crying?" he asked.

"I need to get home but I think I'm lost," she said. "Do you know where Stansbury Road is?"

"Take my hand," he said.

Amy took the boy's cold, little hand and they walked together through the dark forest. She had to walk slowly because his legs were so short. But she didn't mind. It was good to have some company.

"Have you been playing out here today?" she asked, remembering his dirty clothes.

"I've been out here all day," he said. "But not playing."

The boy seemed to know where he was going. Soon they saw a light in the distance.

"Yes!" Amy whispered in joy. "We must be close!"

She squeezed his little hand tighter as they walked toward the light. But as they got closer she saw that they had not come upon a house, but rather a bright lantern sitting near a mound of dirt.

There was a dark, **sinister** figure digging a hole in the ground. They walked up quietly, not getting too close.

"Hey," she whispered. "What's going on?"

The little boy was quiet, standing still. She looked at him and saw that his face was even whiter now,

sinister: suggesting evil.

brilliantly shining against the darkness like a large harvest moon at midnight. Tears started falling from Amy's eyes again as the sound of the shovel hit the dirt in an **eerie** rhythm.

"Where did you bring me?" she asked.

"This is where *it* killed me," was all that the boy said before disappearing down into the very ground he was standing on.

Then the lantern went out, leaving Amy alone in the dark woods with *it*.

[Now SCREAM for your life!]

eerie: weird, scary, spooky.

The Ghost of Jimmie

There was an old **football** field on the east side of Killarney that was said to be haunted. Nobody wanted to play there. The local lads always won because the visiting players spent all their time worrying about seeing the ghost of Jimmie Concannon or, what was almost as bad, actually seeing the ghost of Jimmie Concannon. By the time the game started, them pitiful lads were as sick as a small hospital and so worked up that even their lunches ran a screamin' out of their bodies through the nearest exit, if you know what I mean.

As for why Jimmie Concannon haunted this particular field, nobody knew. Or if they did, they weren't wagging their chins about it. Not to speak ill of the dead, but poor Jimmie was the worst football player that ever was. It was said he was so **feeble**, he couldn't find a green crayon in a box full of green crayons. So maybe he was just trying to get in some extra practice, is all.

football: what people in the United States call soccer.
feeble: very ineffective, weak.

In any case, on this one fierce Saturday afternoon in October, it was, the wind was having its way with the dyin' leaves and there's a game afoot and a brave little **striker** is dribbling the ball down all by his lonesome with only the keeper to beat when suddenly he sees the ghost of Jimmie Concannon, all white and bony he, still in his uni, flesh a droppin' off his face, screaming for the ball.

"I'm open! I'm ooooooopen!" Jimmie wails, shaking his bony arms in the air. "I'm ooooooopen!"

Well, that brave lad's backbone turns to potato soup, it does, and he forgets about the ball and the goal and the fact that Macgillycuddy's Reeks are the tallest mountains in all of Ireland – and come to think of it, wouldn't it be lovely to be takin' a stroll among the clover there right about now, don't you know – and that lad, why, he turns white as, well, he turns white as Jimmy is what he turns, and faints right there on the edge of the goal box.

The following week another brave little lad from a neighborin' brave little county is driving in on net, keeping his head down, hoping against hope not to lose his nerve, when there appears Jimmy again, all white and bony he, with a snake where his tongue should be, up to his usual shenanigans, yelling for the ball.

striker: a forward.

"I'm open! I'm ooooooopen!" he moans, pointing to the spot on the ground in front of his left boot. "I'm ooooooopen!"

Well, that brave lad's legs turn to cabbage stew, they do, and he forgets about the ball and the goal and the fact that Mary had a little lamb – and come to think of it, no one has seen that lamb since McSorley opened his restaurant, don't you know – and that lad, why, his hair turns white as, well, it turns as white as Jimmie is what it turns, and he drops to the **pitch** and curls up like a wee little baby, he does, cryin' for his mother.

So on the last game of the season, it comes down to this for all the potatoes, and the score be tied at **nil** with time a dyin', and here comes this brave lad from another brave little part of the Emerald Isle and, Saints preserve us, if that's not the ghost of Jimmie Concannon standing there, right there to the left of the keeper, all white and bony he, except for the blood-red hair, and he's a callin' for the ball.

"I'm open! I'm ooooooopen!" he groans, a most terrible look in his eye. "I'm ooooooopen!"

Well, that brave lad's heart turns harder than Mrs. O'Leary's week-old soda bread, it does, and he stays focused on the ball and the goal and the fact that shots never taken never find the back o' the net – and come to think of it, wouldn't it be glorious to score in the last minute of play and do a wee little jig for all to see, don't you know – and that brave lad, why, he shoots and... He SCORES!

pitch: field.
nil: nothing; zero.

Ah, 'twas a bleedin'-bloody-brilliant thing to behold, it was.

Shortly thereafter, the referee blows his whistle three times, and it's all over. As the broken-hearted crowd departs the stadium, now a silent graveyard of dead dreams, the only sounds heard are the whoopin' and a hollerin' of the visiting lads as they jump up and down in the middle of the pitch. And Jimmie, poor Jimmie, not at all pleased, is still haunting our hero.

"I was open!" Jimmie cries, cryin' big worm-green tears. "I was ooooooopen! Why did you not pass me the ball, you rotten toadstooooooool?"

[Ending for most U.S. readers:]

"Calm yourself, Jimmie," the lad says with a smile in his voice. "I would have gladly passed you the ball, but I was too scared."

"Scared of meeeeeee?" Jimmie sobs.

"No," the lad says shaking his head. "Scared that you'd miss."

[Ending for True Fans of the Game:]

"Calm yourself, Jimmie," the lad says with a smile in his voice. "I would have gladly passed you the ball, but you were clearly offside."

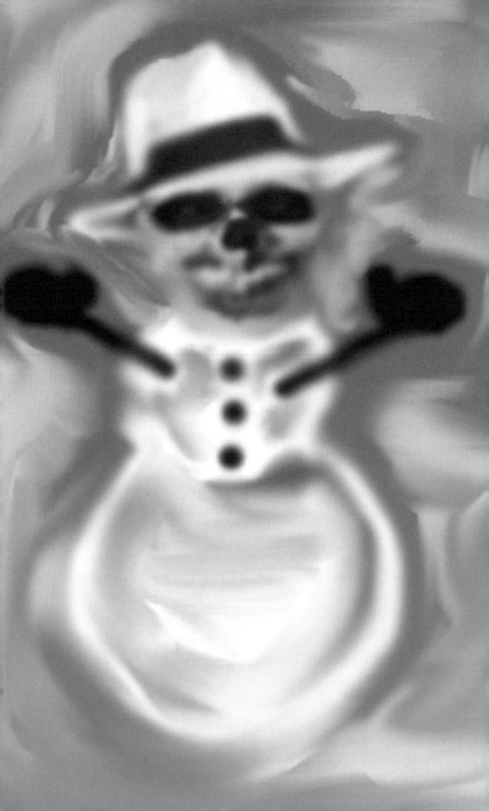

BAD snOMEN

"**A** snowman doesn't have blood coming out of its eyes," Mr. White had said with **disgust** in his voice. "What were you thinking?"

Having recently arrived from Panama, what 7-year-old Carlos was thinking was that he had never seen snow, let alone a snowman. He was also wondering why he had to stay in at recess to write a letter of apology for drawing a green-haired, red-eyed snowman. But his mother had said to listen to the teacher, so the young boy didn't complain and wrote his little letter as best he could.

"mi sorry mi make A BAD sn**OMEN**," it said. "it NO will hapen aGen nOw."

Mr. White threw the letter down on his desk and shook his head. At least it was Friday, he thought.

That day was the last time anyone at the school saw Mr. White. Over the weekend there was a horrible skiing accident. Going full speed, Mr. White flew over a

disgust: a strong feeling of dislike.
omen: a sign of something about to happen.

hill and crashed almost halfway up a tree. Branches as sharp as knives **punctured** both eyes, killing him instantly.

Early Monday morning a scream came from Mr. White's empty room. The other teachers found the principal passed out on the floor by the teacher's desk. In one hand she held the drawing. In the other, the little boy's warning.

punctured: made a hole into.

Checked Out

It was a big, cold house with no television. But Raven's mom always said the same thing.

"Just for an hour. We need to visit Aunt Ruby."

Lately, Aunt Ruby stayed in bed upstairs during the visits. After a little while, her mom would tell Raven to wait downstairs in the library.

The library was large and dusty, with a stench of old, rotting wood. Raven would listen to her music, play with her pocket video game, and hope for the time to tick by quickly.

But one day she began looking at the books on the shelves. She hadn't ever paid much attention to them before and now noticed that they all looked the same, with brown leather covers and gold titles. There were hundreds and hundreds of them that lined three walls of the room. She had heard of some of the books, like *Moby Dick* and *The Great Gatsby*. But as tunes blasted in her ears, she came across one rather strange book on the bottom shelf. She pulled it out.

It looked exactly like the other books, like it had been there for centuries. But the title was different.

Raven Wilson. That was her name! She took the book over to a large chair and opened it. Turning off her music, she started reading the typed print.

October 16: *Raven is born.*

She flipped ahead a little.

April 17: *Grandma dies and Raven pretends to be sad.*

"Hey, who wrote this?" Raven whispered to the book. A **queasy** feeling washed over her. She turned the page and kept reading.

Sept. 22: *Raven breaks lil' Andre's crayons in half. When he starts to cry, she tells him he should be happy because now he has twice as many as before.*

May 29: *Raven gets mad and throws her mom's favorite Nina Simone record on the roof.*

queasy: an upset stomach feeling.

Raven dropped the book into her lap. She was now sweating in the cold house, sweating and feeling like her heart was about to explode because it was pounding so hard. How did anybody know about any of this, and why were they writing it down in a book? Was it Aunt Ruby?

Raven gasped out loud when her mom called from upstairs.

"We're leaving in ten minutes."

Raven felt sweet relief. She had to get out of this house. She turned to the last entry.

January 22: *Raven's mom tells her that they'll be leaving Aunt Ruby's house in ten minutes.*

"How did that happen?" she said, her eyes darting around the room. She looked down again at the last page. But now new words had appeared. Her blood turned into a raging river of ice-cold terror and she started shivering.

January 22: *It's coming for her.*

"Ahhhhhhh!" Raven screamed in her mind.

She tried to get up and run for the door but her legs were **petrified**. Fear gripped her completely. She thought she now heard strange breathing fill the room. But all Raven could do was sit in the

petrified: to be frozen or paralyzed with terror.

chair and look down in horror at the final entry as an **ominous** shadow crept across the book.

January 22: *They will never hear her screams.*

And they didn't.

[Now pause as if the story's over. Then let out a very unexpected SCREAM!]

ominous: threatening.

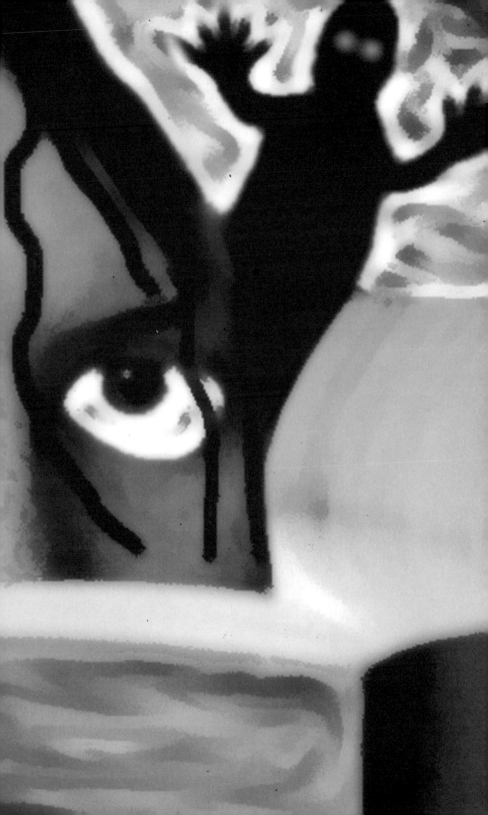

Buried Treasure

The South Will Rise Again Cemetery didn't pay Joe much for doing its dirty work. So Joe **supplemented** his income in the usual way.

It was nasty work digging those holes and filling them again. Joe told himself it wasn't really stealing because those people didn't need their rings, bracelets, necklaces, and watches anymore. They especially didn't need the watches.

"Time's up, suckas," he would whisper to the **corpses** as he helped himself to their belongings.

On this particular late afternoon, Joe – like the sky above – was in a black and dirty mood because "maybees you can't judge no book by 'is cover but you can sure as donkey doo judge a dead man's coin by his box."

In other words, Joe knew that the **probability** of finding something of value under one of these inexpensive pine lids was about the same as his

supplemented: added something to.
corpses: dead bodies.
probability: chance.

chances of winning the lottery. Still, he looked. And to his amazement, the peaceful-looking old man inside the plain, pine coffin had a thick and shiny gold ring on the wrinkled and bony pinky of his right hand.

"Now, grandpa, what you gonna need this here ring fur?" Joe wheezed as he balanced himself on his knees above the old man's open casket.

Joe gave the ring a good tug but nothing happened. So he pulled harder. Again, nothing. The third time he yanked so hard that he lost his balance and fell on top of the old man. Joe's hot, sweaty face squished up against the corpse's cold, dead cheek.

"Get away!" Joe shouted, eyes a bulgin', pushing himself up quickly. "Now you gone and made me mad. Playtime's ovah!"

Joe held onto the ring with both hands, pressed a boot down on the old man's wrist, and pulled so hard he accidentally let out some gas. The ring came off.

But so did the old man's finger!

It flew through the air, end over end, landing among the tombstones.

Joe pocketed the ring and closed the lid – not noticing or caring that the old man had lost his peaceful expression. It had begun to rain and the wind blew through the **decaying** autumn leaves, sending a chill through Joe's moist and smelly

decaying: rotting.

T-shirt. Joe spent all of two seconds looking for the finger but couldn't find it in the dying afternoon light.

"Looky like Rat Christmas come early this year," he said. He moved the mound of dirt into the hole till there was a hole no more. Then he put on his jacket and started for home.

The chubby raindrops got chubbier and the wind blew harder. Joe walked faster and pulled his collar tighter.

By the time he reached his dark and dusty house, Joe was cold through and through. He took a long shower and let the hot water bring back the feeling in his bones. Then he opened a big can of **gumbo** and ate it steaming right out of the pot. He turned on the college football game on his big screen.

An entire pecan pie helped Joe forget about the storm, still raging outside. He had almost forgotten about the ring too.

"Thet's right," he slurred with gumbo and pie crumbs stuck to his chin. "Thet's right."

Then the door bell rang.

"Who be out there on a night like this?" Joe said. "Take your dumb self far away from here."

The door bell rang again. And again. Finally Joe got up, scratched his bulging belly, and cursed all the way to the door. There was no one there. The wild wind blew the roly-poly raindrops into Joe's

gumbo: a southern stew.

face, reminding him why he didn't want to open the door in the first place.

Joe closed the door and went back to the game. But the storm had knocked out the power. Joe was too tired to care. He stumbled down the hall and got into bed.

Outside the rain and wind were now joined by thunder and lightning. And somewhere beyond the storm, a voice began calling. It was an old voice. And it was angry.

"Give me my finger. Give me my fin-geeeeeer," it moaned.

Inside, Joe was too tired to hear. At first.

"I said I want my fin-geeeeeer," it wailed, louder now.

"Yeah, yeah, yeah," Joe said. "I thought I told you to take your dumb self far away from here."

The wind blew harder than ever and the now big, ol', fat-as-**beignet** raindrops beat on Joe's door like one of those dead classic rock drummers and the old man's voice wailed, "Now you made ME mad!"

And Joe's eyes got as big as alligator eggs and he shivered, "Somebody save me."

Then the storm suddenly stopped. Just stopped like someone had flipped a switch or something. It was now as quiet as the grave – something Joe knew about. But a few minutes later, the voice was back and meaner than a sunburned **water moccasin**

beignet: a French doughnut popular in Louisiana.
water moccasin: a type of poisonous snake.

and so close Joe could smell the old man's **putrid** crawfish breath.

"I said I want my FINGER!" it hissed and Joe, who already had the covers pulled over his head, was so scared out of his dim wits that he fainted right then and there in bed before he could call out, "Somebody save me."

The next morning Joe woke up with his finger in his nose. He didn't remember putting it there. But that wasn't all that unusual. (When you're in the buried treasure business, it's hard to turn it off sometimes.) He had a pain behind the eyes but was glad the nightmare had been just that: a nightmare.

Joe picked his nose for a good long while, squinting up at the ceiling, and finally pulled his hand away from his face.

Horror-struck, he realized that both his hands were already down on the bed. Then he looked at his favorite nose-picking hand. There was only a white, bloody stump where his pinky should have been.

With his **severed** finger still wiggling around in his nose, Joe ran screaming out into the street in just his underwear.

In a stuffy-nose voice he just kept shouting, "Somebody save me! Somebody save me! Somebody save me!"

putrid: rotting.
horror-struck: filled with fear.
severed: cut off; separated.

El Cuco

El *Cuco* comes for children who don't listen to their parents," Juan told Little Johnny again as he kissed his son good night. "*El Cuco* comes for children who stay up past their bedtime. Be strong, my son. Be good."

It was the same story that Juan's father had told him when he was a child. Thousands and thousands of Spanish-speaking children went to bed each night with the story of *El Cuco*. But here in the United States of America you were not supposed to tell such things to little children. The counselors and psychologists said it was not healthy. And Juan's wife agreed.

"Juan, please stop telling him that cuckoo story," she said. "I don't want Little Johnny to have nightmares."

"Yes, dear," Juan said.

Juan loved his son very much and didn't want him to become a mama's boy, *un nene de mamá*.

He knew the world was sometimes a cold, hard place and that Little Johnny would have to learn to be tough and hard too. He wanted him to be strong, strong on the inside. But Juan was losing the battle.

Little Johnny wasn't strong. He was soft and flabby and gooey on the inside. He was *un llorón de primera*. A world-class cry baby. Always crying to his mother about every little thing.

"*El Cuco* lives in that hole in the wall over there," Juan told Little Johnny the next night. "He waits for *niños malos* – bad children – and then he comes out for them. Be strong, my son. Be good."

A few minutes later, Little Johnny was knocking on his parent's bedroom door.

"Daddy told me the cuckoo would get me," he cried. "He said it would come out of the hole in the wall."

"Poor baby," his mother said, hugging Little Johnny tightly and giving Juan a dark look. "Silly Daddy will patch that hole and that mean cuckoo won't be able to get you."

The next morning Juan got his **putty knife**, mixed some **plaster**, and covered the little hole in the wall. He then painted over it, so that no one would ever be able to tell there had been a hole in the first place.

"The hole is gone," Juan told Little Johnny that night. "But *El Cuco* is still there. Be strong, my son. Be good."

---

putty knife: a hand tool used to mix or spread soft mixtures.
plaster: a mixture used to cover or repair walls and ceilings.

"No, you said it lives in the hole and the hole is gone," Little Johnny said. "No more cuckoo."

"Be careful what you say," Juan warned. "The only way to keep *El Cuco* away is to be strong, to be good."

"Cuckoo all gone," Little Johnny teased as he jumped and danced on the bed. "Cuckoo can't get me. Cuckoo can't get me."

That night Little Johnny heard a muffled sound coming from inside the wall where the hole used to be.

"I'm coming for you, *niño malo*," a voice said. There was scratching and pounding and pounding and scratching as plaster and dust and dust and plaster fell from the wall.

Little Johnny was too scared to look, too scared to cry, too scared even to wet the bed.

"I don't like bad little boys," the voice said, now free from the wall. "You should have listened to your *papá*. *Pero es demasiado tarde ahora.* It's too late now.

"Oh, you know what else I don't like?" the voice whispered into Little Johnny's terrified ear. "I really don't like to be called cuckoo. My name is *El Cuco!*"

El Cuco opened up a large sack filled with other bad children and dropped Little Johnny inside.

Then he was gone.

The next morning Little Johnny was gone too. But the hole in the wall was back.

Hot Heads
of Jalapeño Canyon

"It get hot up there," the old man had warned them at the gas station. "I would not go there today if I was *chu*."

The four college buddies had rolled their eyes at each other and made the international sign for *loco de la cabeza*. When they got to the **trailhead**, the hikers loaded their packs and quickly put five miles behind them. The top of Mt. Gato Anaranjado was now just two miles away.

"Piece of cake," one of them said. "*Chu* would have to agree."

They all laughed. And their laughter echoed up and back down the canyon.

Back at the gas station, the old man was laughing too. He was laughing because he knew things. He knew, for example, that…

[Now start laughing and don't stop until your listeners start laughing too. Then stop laughing and

trailhead: the point where a trail begins.

pretend the story is over. When your friends ask questions or complain that the story wasn't scary, grab one of them and scream like you're insane.]

Sometimes the scariest thing about a story is the person who is telling it. Another way to tell this rather silly tale is to read it twice. Then just wait. When someone says something – and they always do – just start repeating whatever they say. Do this for a while, and when the person starts getting tired or annoyed, just SCREAM!

The Man in the Box

The last thing I remember is being out in a field with the wind and sun hitting my face. And then nothing. No memory, only darkness.

I don't know how long I've been in this box. It is as dark as the grave in here and impossible to breathe.

At least I am not alone. My eyes are useless but I can feel others in here and smell their sick, sweet, banana-maple fear. In the blackness I hear their voices.

One of them keeps saying how you don't want to leave this box. He must be crazy. I dream about it every night: getting out, getting out, getting out.

"Escape is death and death is escape," he repeats, making no sense that I can see. Of course, I cannot see anything.

He whispers that he has heard the cries of the victims when the end comes.

"The sound of thick water, gasping, and screams," the voice screeches. "The killer uses a giant shovel and then the lights go out... *forever*."

"I don't want to die! I don't want to die!" I hear the screaming coming from inside my head.

Suddenly everything starts to shake and at first I'm afraid that it's an earthquake and then, yes, it has to be an earthquake and maybe, just maybe, if it's a big one and I survive, maybe some way, somehow I'll be thrown clear and... escape!

And then I see the light. The light! The wonderful, glorious light! And I am filled with fear and joy and joy and joy and shaking and then I hear the thunder speak.

"BREAKFAST, MIKEY. I GOT YOU YOUR FAVORITE CEREAL!!!"

Eyes drowning in white light, lungs in white water, my scream is lost among so many. I see the shovel now coming toward me and close my eyes. And close my eyes...

Ol' Fish Brains

Ahoy, maties. Gather round and see if ye can stomach this tale of the sea. If ye have the spine for it, aye. For this here be the tale of Ol' Fish Brains, it be. Yo, ho, ho and a bottle of clam juice.

Arr…

'Tis no great mystery why the men of the Stella called him Ol' Fish Brains neither.

"Save me the heads, Cookie," he would whisper to the cook with a black look in his one good eye. "The heads."

He would pop out the eyes of the raw fish heads with his rotting teeth and chomp on 'em like they be gum and then suck out the brains through the empty eye sockets.

And there he'd be all a slurpin' and a smilin' with fish blood and brain juice running down his beard. Arr. Sometimes pieces, sometimes whole eyeballs would drop down into that beard and the eyes would look out at you and you'd swear that they could see

right through you and every sin that ever stained yer soul. Aye.

'Twas all he would eat. Real picky that way, he was.

Arr, sure enough that Ol' Fish Brains 'twas a crazy, old seabird. There be no question of that, maties. He blew his nose on his shirt and sometimes forgot to wear his eyepatch to cover the ugly hole where his eye used to be before he rubbed it out of his head after an extra crusty biscuit crumb got in there.

But he talked of the map and the buried treasure so often that some among the crew started to believe. Not that they would admit to it, aye, but in their lonely bunks with only the lice for company, they dreamed of those gold coins, those gold coins that increased in number every time the ol' crow told the tale.

One night, four weeks out at sea, it was, these two **unsavory** buckos break into the last rum barrel on board and start a drinkin' and a talkin'. A talkin' and a drinkin'. Talkin' about the treasure.

Arr.

"I know where he keeps that map," the one says to the other. "'Twould be an easy thing."

So they set a plannin' the deed for the next night when Ol' Fish Brains be asleep in his bunk. But the ol' bird wakes up and pulls a knife. A terrible **ruckus ensues** and the next thing anyone knows,

unsavory: morally bad; not pleasing in smell or taste.
ruckus: the act of making a noisy disturbance.
ensues: follows.

Ol' Fish Brains has the blade stickin' out of his one good eye and right before he dies, he sits up and yells, "Save me the heads!"

Arr. Well, nobody saw who did it. Or else nobody was willin' to say. Anyways, everyone from the captain to the cook felt more at ease now that Ol' Fish Brains was gone.

Aye. A quick prayer, over the side of the ship, and gone to **Davy Jones' locker** was he. Glug, glug, glug. Gone. Arr.

It was a still, black night three weeks later. No stars nor moon cut through the drippin' fog. Not a drop of wind in all the sea and a quiet, an eerie quiet, hung over the port. Aye. A creepy feelin' come in from the water all dark and dead like.

And 'twas then that they saw her out in the water. The Stella, it had to be. No life blowin' in her ragged sails, just hanging there all **akimbo**. But somehow she was movin' closer and closer to shore.

And when she came closer still, they could see the crew standing on deck. The first mate grippin' the wheel. The captain next to him. Aye. Not a sound they made moving through the water on that terrible night.

And then as she came even closer, some among the crowd let out a gasp. Others a scream. Some made no sound, just fainted. Others still ran back to the town, to the hills. It didn't seem to matter where. Aye.

Davy Jones' locker: the bottom of the sea; death.
akimbo: bent, crooked; hands on hips, arms bent at elbows.

For the men of the Stella were all missing their heads, ya see. Every last one of 'em. Not a head among the whole lot, aye.

Dead men tell no tales, so the few landlubbers who still had their wits about them were left with many a question but few answers. How did the Stella make its way back to port with a dead crew? How could the ship move with no wind in her sails? And what happened to the men and their heads?

Well, they never found the heads of the sailors of the Stella. Arr. Some say the ghost of Ol' Fish Brains took 'em. But that can't be. After all, there be no such thing as ghosts.

Arr! Hahahahahahahahahahaaaaaa! Arr!

Welcome to the Neighborhood

Farewell Bend Cemetery was on the outskirts of town. It was a pioneer cemetery, and most of the graves were well over a hundred years old. Some of the people who had built the little town were buried there too, Mrs. Bunk had told the class. The graveyard was full of history.

The class of 28 fourth graders stood in front of the gates of the cemetery. This was one crazy field trip, Allen Rivers thought. And the trip over was crazy too. Because the cemetery was only a few blocks away from the school, the class had walked instead of taking a bus. They had to walk along the busy highway that cut through the middle of town, but they all made it to the cemetery safely.

Mrs. Bunk began to talk about the pioneers and all the hardships they went through on their journey out west, but Allen wasn't listening. He was getting his camera out of his backpack. His grandpa had given him an ancient camera last week and this would be a perfect place to try it out. It was even loaded with a roll of film, just like in the old days. He was excited that he would be able to use this creepy camera in this creepy place.

When Mrs. Bunk stopped talking, the kids were allowed to wander around and read the **epitaphs**. Allen ran through the cemetery like a wild horse, taking pictures of his classmates and yelling "look this way, this way" over and over again.

Then Allen ran up to a large, moss-covered tombstone where a girl was standing by herself.

"Hey," he yelled, "let me take your picture with that cool tombstone."

The girl didn't answer. He didn't recognize her, but maybe she was a new student. Or maybe she was visiting the cemetery with her parents.

"Don't be such a grump!" Allen said. "You might as well look this way." Click. "Ha! That will show you. I got your picture!"

The girl wore a **somber** expression and stared at Allen with large, black eyes. He backed away, but her hate-filled glare followed him. He then turned from her and ran, but he could still feel the girl's eyes on his back all the way across the cemetery. It wasn't until he got to the front gate and rejoined his friends that he felt those piercing eyes were finally off him. Sure enough, when he turned around, he saw that the girl was gone.

epitaphs: the words written on tombstones.
somber: dark; sad; serious.

The students sat on the grass and ate lunch from brown paper bags. Allen nervously looked around for the new girl but couldn't find her anywhere. He was actually happy when Mrs. Bunk told them they were heading back to school. This place was giving him the creeps.

The class walked single file along the busy traffic of the highway. It was loud. Allen couldn't wait to give his mom the roll of film that he had finished and get his pictures developed. Maybe he could bring them to school the next day.

Suddenly the hairs on the back of his neck stood up. That strange girl in the cemetery – those dark, terrible eyes – he could sense her watching him again even though the graveyard was far behind them now.

A sick feeling flooded his stomach. Allen turned around, but she wasn't there. Still not convinced, he stepped out onto the road to get a better look.

The truck driver had no time to stop. Allen Rivers died instantly. Somehow the old camera survived the accident, landing in a nearby field.

Months later Allen's mother took the film in and had it developed. Although it was hard for her to look at the photographs of classmates posing and smiling in the graveyard, it did make her happy that Allen had a fun day. But then she came across the very last picture. She let out a tortured scream and then fainted on the spot.

Standing next to a large, mossy tombstone, a **wraith**-like little girl was staring straight into the camera with the most evil, dark eyes. But that wasn't the worst part. The worst part was that the tombstone read *Allen Rivers, Rest in Peace.*

wraith: a type of ghost.

Ghost Dogs

"On nights like these the dogs come out and take their revenge," Larry told the other two boys as they sat around the campfire. "That's what some of the old Indians say, anyway."

The three friends were squeezing in one more backpacking trip before going back to school. A freezing wind blew in off the river, blowing smoke and **embers** everywhere. The full moon disappeared behind some clouds.

Larry, who was a little older, had just finished telling the yawning Dixon brothers about how the men of the Lewis and Clark expedition barely survived their trip through the Bitterroot Mountains of Idaho. Half-frozen and half-starving, the **Corps of Discovery** stumbled into a Nez Perce village just in time.

The Indians shared their salmon and roots with the travelers. But after stuffing themselves, the explorers got picky.

embers: the coal or ash of a dying fire.
Corps of Discovery: name of the Lewis and Clark exploration team.

As they made their way down the Columbia River, Lewis and Clark would stop at every village along the way and trade the Native Americans for their dogs. All the Indians could do was shake their heads at these very strange strangers.

"Surrounded by all that delicious, pink salmon flesh and these guys ate dogs," Larry said. "You can understand why the ghosts of Spot, Fido, and Lassie might be a wee bit upset."

The brothers weren't sure if they should believe Larry, even though he was the history nerd of the group.

"Nah-uh," Simon was about to say when something wet and cold licked his nose. It had started to snow. Big, heavy flakes fell from the September night, a little early for snow but the mountains are like that.

"'Night, losers," Larry called to the brothers as they went in their tent.

A few minutes later Simon was sleeping like a smelly baby, and in the other tent Larry was snoring up a storm of his own. Meanwhile, Danny shivered inside his cheap sleeping bag and wondered if he'd ever be able to get warm.

Sometime during the night – he couldn't tell how much time had gone by or if he'd slept at all – Danny heard what sounded like dogs howling. Or was it the wind and his tired mind playing tricks on him?

But a few minutes later, there it was again, louder and closer. He heard the howling just as clearly as he heard Larry snoring a few feet away. The dogs – or whatever it was – made a sad, mournful sound. Through it all, Simon kept sleeping and Danny was once again amazed at how his brother could snooze through anything. The snow kept falling, sticking to the tent until it got too heavy and then rolling off in clumps. Danny poked his head out but didn't see anything except for all that snow.

At some point, Danny passed out and finally slept. He could still hear the dogs in his dreams.

The next morning a half foot of soft snow covered everything. Danny got up first and then Simon. Larry had finally stopped snoring.

"That was some dumb, boring story Larry was trying to sell us last night, huh?" Simon said, stretching.

The brothers had breakfast and packed up their gear. But Larry still hadn't gotten up.

"Hey, Sleeping Beauty, time to get a move on," Simon said finally. Danny threw a snowball at Larry's tent. And then he noticed that the snow around the bottom of the tent wasn't white. It was dark. Red even.

Worried now, Danny stuck his head inside the tent. Larry looked like he had been ripped apart by wolves. Or dogs. What was left of him looked like the pink salmon flesh he had talked about the night before. There was animal hair mixed in with everything too.

Danny screamed and then Simon looked in the tent and he screamed too. And then they screamed together. And then they screamed some more. It would take a lot more screaming before the brothers realized that there weren't any animal tracks anywhere near Larry's tent. All that soft, fresh snow and not one single paw print.

The boys just kept screaming.

[Now scream. Hopefully your listeners will join you. Just keep screaming together, or alone. Just keep screaming…]

Larry's account of the Lewis and Clark expedition is true. The explorers really did prefer to eat dog meat rather than fish, even though they were in the salmon capital of the world. They also preferred dog meat to horsemeat, which they were forced to eat sometimes.

By the way, cases of wolves attacking humans are quite rare. A healthy wild wolf has not killed anyone in the United States in the last 50 years. Dogs, on the other hand, killed 32 Americans in 2007 alone.

A Real Bad Burrito

Jim felt himself floating above the overturned car. Even as it still slid down the black icy road, he could somehow see the driver through the twisted metal and broken glass. At first Jim couldn't see the dead man's face. But then the corpse slowly turned its head, opened its eyes, and stared straight up at Jim. Through the fog in his mind, Jim recognized the face. It was his face.

"Ahhhhhhhhhhhhhhhh!"

Jim woke up screaming, his pillow wet under his head. He **inhaled** deeply and let the fact sink in that it had only been a dream.

"Okay, no more midnight burritos for you, buddy," he told himself. But the nightmare had been too real to laugh away. As he stood at the top of the stairs, Jim made a decision. "Maybe it was a warning. Maybe the dream was trying to tell me I shouldn't drive into town today."

inhaled: breathed in.

Jim didn't see his toddler's toy car on the second step. Suddenly he lost his balance and began tumbling down the stairs. He didn't stop till he reached the bottom. By then it was too late. Jim's neck was twisted in a way necks are not supposed to twist. His lifeless eyes stared out into space, seeing only emptiness.

Next to his body, the overturned toy car was still spinning.

Pumpkin Eye

By the time they made it out to the pumpkin patch, the sun was low in the sky.

"I can't wait to tell the kids at school about this," said María as she squeezed the large, yellow flashlight she had brought from her garage.

"Yeah, this will be cool," said Adriana. They both had backpacks filled with blankets, snacks, and cameras. It might be a long night and they were ready.

The pumpkin patch was out in the country, surrounded by cornfields and next to an old, **rickety** house that was barely standing. Few people came out here anymore – not since the slick, new pumpkin patch, complete with free hay rides and hot cider, opened on the other side of town.

But María and Adriana weren't there to buy a pumpkin. They were there to see the ghost of Robby Bligh, a teenager who had died in that very field over 20 years ago. According to the stories, Robby

rickety: likely to break or fall apart; shaky.

could be seen haunting the patch during autumn nights.

Nobody was around, except for the pumpkins. It was quiet and cold as the sun disappeared. The girls could see their foggy breaths hang in the air when they whispered to each other.

"Ready here," said María, pressing buttons on the video camera she had borrowed from her mom. "Now that Robby just needs to show and we'll be Internet stars, girl!"

Adriana laughed.

"Did you hear that?" Adriana whispered.

The distant sound of dry leaves crunching pierced the still night. As a matter of fact, María had heard it too and her arms turned all chicken skin.

"Someone's coming this way, but I don't see anyone," María said.

"Someone or *something*," said Adriana.

The sound grew louder as the two girls stared into the darkness, their hearts beating crazy hard. Something was walking right toward them. Suddenly they could see a tall, thin figure just a few feet away. Then, to their horror, it spoke.

"Ooohhhhhhhhhhhh."

The voice sounded old and hollow and the girls screamed and took off running. The footsteps followed them, and the girls could swear they heard Robby Bligh at their heels, yelling out to them, angry and seeking revenge.

"Don't run! Don't ruuuuuun!"

But María and Adriana ran like a five-legged **puma**. They ran and ran until María let out a terrifying, horrible scream and disappeared from Adriana's side. Adriana stopped and turned around, desperately calling and looking for her friend, but couldn't find her. María had disappeared.

Adriana ran all the way home and told her parents what had happened. Later when the paramedics found María lying in the dirt, an old, thin man was with her.

"I live in the house over yonder and this here's my pumpkin patch," the old man explained to the paramedics as they were putting a bandage around María's bloody head.

"I tried to tell them youngsters not to run in the pumpkin patch, that it's dangerous, but they took off anyway."

He cleared the old-man **phlegm** from his throat.

"You know, that's how that fella Robby Bligh died out here some years back. He was running through the pumpkins and tripped and fell head first right into the biggest pumpkin we had ever grown. The stem went clear through his eye socket and into his brain, killing him on the spot.

"This gal here's just lucky. That little pumpkin just bloodied her up a bit. What you need two eyes for anyway?"

puma: also known as a cougar, mountain lion, or panther.
phlegm: saliva mixed with mucus.

Room for Two More

Ted and Wendy passed through mile after mile of the most **epic** winter wonderland. The sky above was a brilliant blue, and the snow was not too soft and not too hard. Even Goldilocks would have said it was just right. The two snowshoers were heading toward a place on the map called *Satan's Lava Flow*.

"This is amazing but, dude, I'm so hungry I would sell my soul for a brownie," Ted said after a few hours.

Just then they saw smoke in the distance. A fire, they both thought. It would be sweet to warm themselves by a fire while they ate lunch. After a few more minutes, they came to a cabin-like shelter.

"According to the map, this isn't supposed to be here," Ted said.

"Well, I'm going in," Wendy said. "You can stay out here and eat your map."

epic: very large, powerful, or wonderful; awesome.

It was dark and smoky inside. Old, **rustic** benches surrounded a black wood stove. When their eyes adjusted to the darkness, Wendy and Ted saw that they were not alone.

A man sat huddled in the darkest corner of the shelter. A tattered, red wool blanket pulled tightly around his head made it hard to see his face except for his hollow, tired eyes, which looked out in the distance.

Ted said hello but the man didn't answer. The man's presence seriously weirded them out, so they quickly chomped down their lunch and said good-bye. Once again the man didn't answer.

Then just as they were about to leave, he suddenly turned toward them and those dead eyes came to life with an evil, dark glow that **illuminated** the shelter and threw dark shadows into their souls. He seemed to speak to them without words, and the things he said filled Ted and Wendy with a cold that had nothing to do with the temperature.

They quickly put on their snowshoes and headed back into the woods. Ted turned around once and thought he saw the entire hut glowing with that horrible, dark light. Wendy could have sworn she heard terrible laughter coming from its direction. They quickly crunched through the woods in silence. Ted finally spoke.

"Man, that guy was creepy."

rustic: rough or unfinished.
illuminated: lighted.

"No duh," Wendy said. "Did you see how he looked at us?"

The short winter day was getting shorter and a storm was moving in. Fortunately the snowshoers saw a sign that told them they were just two miles from their car.

"Almost there," Ted said.

"Almost there," Wendy said.

A dark wind began ripping through the trees, knocking down huge icicles from the branches. The sky was now the color of snow and their legs began to ache.

After an hour they came to another sign. Ted studied the sign through **weary** eyes and then studied it some more.

"According to this we're still two miles from the parking lot," Ted sighed. "I don't understand it."

He was sure they had made all the right turns at all the right places. A sick feeling gripped his **bowels** at the next intersection. There, another sign told them they were no closer to the car.

"Okay, someone's playing a joke," Wendy said. "Maybe somebody switched all the signs."

Snow began to fall sideways as Ted pulled the map and compass out of his pack.

"Forget those dumb signs," he said in a shaky voice. "If we start heading north, we're bound to reach the parking lot or at least the highway."

weary: tired.
bowels: intestines; guts.

Horror-struck, he saw the compass needle spinning madly. Round and round it went. Ted yelled and threw the compass against a nearby tree. Then, too tired to hold the anger, he dropped to his knees.

Which way was north? Everything looked the same. No landmarks. Just trees in every direction. Wendy wondered how things had turned so bad so fast. The wind was blowing harder now, the snow sticking to the trees like the fear that began to coat their insides. And it was getting cold. Very cold.

"We've got to s-s-start moving," Ted said through chattering teeth. They patted each other on the shoulders the way football players do before a game.

"We can do this," Ted said.

"We can do this!" Wendy shouted back.

An hour later the sky had disappeared behind the screaming snow and it was getting harder and harder to see. Still, with legs of lead they plowed on.

"I'm tired," Wendy whispered a few minutes later. "So tired. Wait... Do you smell that?"

It was the strong smell of blackened wood, like a fire after the fire has gone out. Somehow the shelter must be close by, Ted thought. They could get warm and rest and get out of the storm. Through the driving snow, they could barely make out the outline of the wooden **structure**. The last of their energy gone, they smiled weakly at each other and shuffled toward it. Then they stopped dead in their tracks.

The man was still there. Ted saw those evil eyes, looking past the snow and the darkness, looking into him. And Wendy heard the laughter again. *That terrible laughter.*

They went inside.

[Laugh your most crazy-sounding laugh while making crazy eyes at your audience.]

structure: something constructed, like a building.

Meat Me in the Cafeteria

It all started with burgers.

After years of the most gruesome, gut-wrenching **grub** known to child and man, the cafeteria at Mission Viejo Elementary, suddenly and most unexpectedly, one day began serving the best burgers in the world. Fresh, juicy, fat, charbroiled, teachers-running-in-the-hall-with-scissors, crazy good burgers!

There was no chance of a food fight breaking out on the days these babies were handed out.

But then a strange thing started happening. The kids at Mission Viejo Elementary began to get old. No, not older like an eight-year-old waking up on their birthday morning and being nine. The kids at Mission Viejo Elementary were getting real old, real fast.

Little first graders with white hair. Wrinkled up third graders with bad knees. Fifth graders with **dentures**.

grub: food.
dentures: false teeth.

And then it became known that the company selling the burgers to the school was getting its meat from something other than cows.

To save money the company had been stealing bodies from nursing homes and cemeteries and turning them into... burgers. Fresh, juicy, fat, charbroiled, teachers-running-in-the-hall-with-scissors, crazy good burgers!

After that, salads became much more popular at Mission **Viejo** Elementary.

viejo: *old* in Spanish.

The Old Woman

Many years ago now, when I was a little boy, my grandfather he say to me this story.

Long before the railroad and the automobile and the jet plane, there was the canoe and the **voyageurs**. Transporting the beaver fur from the vast Canadian wilderness through dangerous rivers, windy lakes, and hungry mosquitoes was the work of the men of the north. My grandfather was one such man.

On this particular trip coming back down the river Churchill heavy with beaver skins, a new paddler he joined my grandfather's crew. Now Julien LeCoq he put his back into the long day of paddling and **portaging** and portaging and paddling. And the boss he say Julien LeCoq could run the rapids that would make other men go poo poo in their *pantalon*.

Still, the other men did not like Julien LeCoq. There was something about him, though what it was

voyageurs: boatmen, woodsmen, trappers, or explorers hired by fur companies in Canada hundreds of years ago.
portaging: carrying boats and supplies between lakes or rivers.

for sure *mon grand pere*, my grandfather, he could not say. Perhaps it was that he paddled silently, not singing like the other men. Or *se possible* it was the way he was always looking around with large, nervous eyes, like he was waiting for something to happen.

Nobody had ever seen eyes like the eyes of Julien LeCoq.

As the voyage she go on, Julien LeCoq began to act more and more **bizarre**. He stopped sleeping and began talking about *la vieille femme*, the old woman. Always *la vieille femme*.

"The old woman" was the name the voyageurs gave to the wind. You see, the wind she is the great enemy of the man who travels by canoe.

[Make wind sounds.]

One night Julien LeCoq began to whisper, "*La vieille femme vient pour moi. Le mort vient pour moi.* The old woman she is coming for me. Death she is coming for me."

And the next day Julien LeCoq he began to **croon**.

"*La vieille femme vient pour moi! Le mort vient pour moi!*" he sang in a high, shaky voice as he paddled. "The old woman she is coming for me. Death she is coming for me."

[Make wind sounds.]

bizarre: strange, odd.
croon: to sing softly.

The trip and Julien they continue in this fashion for many days and nights with the sleepless **obsession** of *la vieille femme*.

Finalement, finally you would say, one night the group is on a little island at the end of a huge lake and the wind she begin to blow with great anger. The lake was a terrible ocean of waves. It was useless to try and make the fire. The men they were happy to have a break from the mosquito and the black fly, but they were no so happy to have no hot food.

[Make wind sounds.]

One of the men, trying only to have a little fun, he say to Julien, "The old woman she is blowing tonight, no, Julien? The big lake is quite angry. Heh, heh, heh."

But Julien, his eyes all *rouge* – how you say? red – he fail to see the humor and threw himself on the man, screaming "*La vieille femme vient pour moi! Le mort vient pour moi!*" He would have killed that man if the others had not pulled him off.

My grandfather he did his best to calm down the poor fellow. He say to him, "*C'est seulement le vent*, Julien. It is only the wind."

But it was no use. Julien LeCoq he pulled away and ran into the woods behind the camp, screaming as he went.

---

obsession: spending too much time thinking about something.

"La vieille femme vient pour moi! Le mort vient pour moi! The old woman she is coming for meeeeee..."

And then his tortured voice it disappeared into the black night and the crying of the old woman.

[Make wind sounds.]

The next morning the wind she is gone and Julien he no return. The other men say, "Yoohoo, Julien? Where are you? Where are you hiding to? Yoohoo, Julien?"

Julien still he had to be on the little island. But after searching and searching, they could not find him.

And so the voyage she go on without Julien LeCoq.

The voyageurs paddled all day to cross the giant lake, not even stopping once to smoke the pipe. As they were approaching the far shore, each man thought he could hear the whispering of Julian LeCoq. It was only their imagination. That is what they say to themselves.

"La vieille femme vient pour moi. Le mort vient pour moi."

[Make wind sounds.]

And then they saw him – or what was left of him – sitting against a big rock. The unforgettable eyes staring out at the sky, staring out from the skeleton of Julian LeCoq! All that was left were those eyes still in the skull and the bones, bones burned and black as the night.

There was no sign of a campfire, and there was no explanation for how Julien LeCoq could have crossed that gigantic lake.

Though **exhausted**, the men paddled long into the darkness that silent night. Through all the miles and all the years after that, my grandfather he was never able to forget the song of Julien LeCoq.

"*La vieille femme vient pour moi. Le mort vient pour moi.*"

Listen. Do you not hear?

The old woman she is dancing tonight.

[Make wind sounds.]

La vieille femme vient pour moi...

[Make wind sounds.]

[Suddenly turn to someone and shout] *Et pour VOUS*!!!

exhausted: very tired.
et pour vous: *and for you* in French.

Wack-O

The strange man with the **deranged** look in his eyes hid behind a tree. Running down the wooded river trail, Ed never knew what hit him. In a crazed split second, the man swung at Ed like Big Papi going for the fences. Wack-O! The huge branch exploded into the back of Ed's head and everything went black.

He was in a coma for three weeks and very nearly died. They never caught the man behind the tree.

After a long, painful recovery, Ed's life went back to normal. He even began running again.

One beautiful Sunday morning, Ed decided to go back to his favorite trail, the one where it had happened. At first Ed was troubled by the memory of that day and his heart raced ahead of his running shoes. But after a few minutes, the sights and sounds of spring filled his senses with the present. It was a new day. And it was great to be alive.

deranged: crazy, insane.

Ed ran hard and fast and felt the power returning to his body like an extinct volcano finding its magma again. Then he noticed the laces on his left shoe had come undone. He stopped behind a tree and... something happened. His eyes rolled back in his head, the color left his face, and the edges of his mouth turned up slightly into a threatening, sick smile.

Behind the tree, Ed waited patiently – with a heavy branch in his hand – for the next runner to pass.

Problem Number 13

Most of the babysitters in town wouldn't go near the house on Carney Hill. But Eliza was new in Big Top, so she hadn't heard the stories. All she knew was that Mr. and Mrs. Kerr needed a babysitter, and she needed the money.

The Kerrs and their three children seemed friendly enough. So what if the house was decorated with dozens of clown paintings? Eliza wasn't afraid of clowns. She couldn't understand why so many kids were.

"Joe and I will be back around 10 o'clock," said Mrs. Kerr. "Make sure the kids get to bed by nine."

The well-behaved children drew pictures quietly, mostly of clowns, and then watched an old black-and-white TV show called *Circus Boy* until it was bedtime.

After the kids were all in their beds, the babysitter **reluctantly** began doing her math homework under a giant painting which hung over the fireplace.

A few minutes later, Eliza glanced up from her work and noticed that the sad clown in the painting seemed to be looking at her. Nonsense, she thought. It was just that she was sitting right in the clown's line of sight. Still, she took her books and went over to the other side of the room.

When Eliza finished her homework, she looked up again at the painting. No. It couldn't be. The clown was looking right at her!

Eliza shut her eyes so tightly they felt like they were going to pop out of her head. Then suddenly she heard the children screaming and she ran upstairs toward the bedrooms. Out of the corner of her eye, she could have sworn she saw that the clown was no longer in the painting.

At the top of the stairs, Eliza froze. There, standing right in front of her, was the clown from the painting.

"How's the math going?" he laughed. "I've been watching you all night."

His large, red shoes began moving towards her and then he whispered, "I think you got problem number 12 wrong."

The last thing to come from Eliza's lips was a **bloodcurdling** scream. Then the lights went out at the house on Carney Hill.

reluctantly: showing or feeling no excitement over doing something.
bloodcurdling: terrifying.

The children were not able to explain what had happened and the police never found Eliza.

In all the confusion, no one noticed that Eliza had missed just one math problem – the last one, problem 12. And somehow no one noticed that the sad clown in the giant painting over the fireplace was no longer sad. Finally, no one noticed that there was something reflected in the clown's eyes: It was a girl. And she was screaming.

[Now scream.]

I Doooooooooooooo...

Dan's knees shook like leaves on a windy day.

"Focus, Dan, focus," he told himself.

Dan had never gotten over his fear of heights. He had just learned to control it by paying attention to the small details of his job. For the last several years, Dan had been a window washer, hanging off the side of some of the tallest buildings in town.

"Wet it down," Dan reminded himself. "Now use the squeegee."

But Dan's knees weren't shaking on this day because he was hundreds of feet off the ground. He was shaking because he was excited. Linda worked on the top floor of this building. And tonight after work, he was going to ask Linda to marry him.

As Dan was working on the floor below Linda's office, he reached into his pocket to look at the ring he had bought her.

"I hope she says *yes*," he said out loud.

Suddenly the ring slipped out of Dan's sweaty hand. It bounced off the **scaffold** he was standing on and landed on the ledge of the building. He tried to reach it but his safety harness didn't let him. There was only one thing to do. Dan removed the harness and stretched for the ring.

Just as he grabbed it, a powerful gust of wind hit. The scaffold swayed violently. Dan lost his balance and fell over the side.

Dan found himself hanging from the bottom of the platform by the fingers of his left hand. His feet danced below him high above the busy street. Somehow, he was still squeezing his right fist around the ring.

With his heart screaming in his ears, Dan quickly put the ring in his pocket and grabbed hold with both hands. Using all his strength, he pulled himself back onto the scaffold and into his harness.

"That was close," Dan said, trying to catch his breath. "But it's all good now."

A few minutes later, Dan happily pounded on the window glass to get Linda's attention. She didn't hear him, so he pounded harder. Again she didn't hear. He started hitting the window so hard he thought the glass would break.

Finally, Linda looked up from her work and came toward the window where Dan was waving now. A

---

scaffold: a platform on which a person stands while working off the ground.

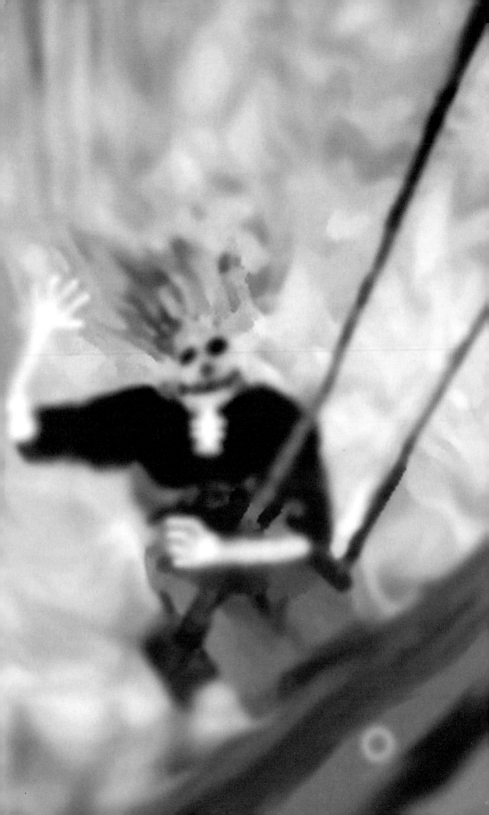

look of horror filled her face. She turned pale and crashed to the floor.

"Linda!" Dan screamed. "Lindaaaaaaaaaa!"

Linda's best friend Barbara, who had heard the noise from next door, helped Linda up to a nearby chair.

"It was Dan, wasn't it?" Barbara asked.

"Yes," Linda said through her sobbing. "He came back just like he always does each year on this day. The day 13 years ago when he fell to his death."

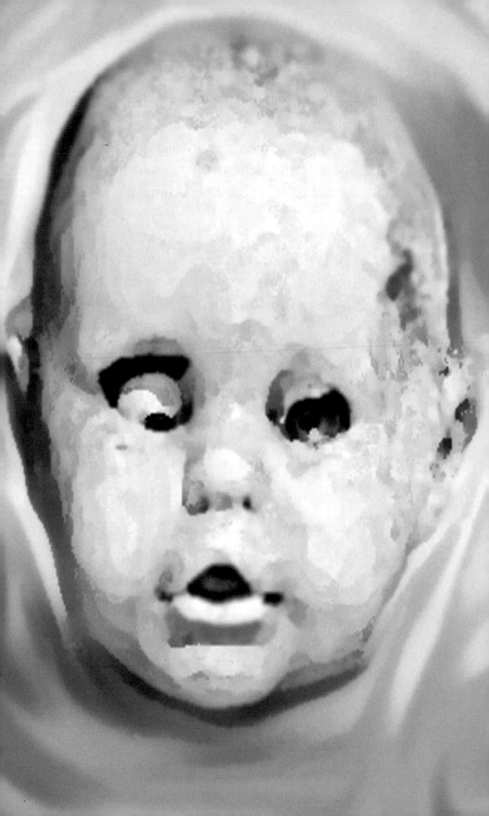

Don't Forget to Flush

Jesse Jones hated that *stooopid* little doll as much as he hated his *stooopid* little sister.

She was always getting him in trouble. (Although if truth be known, Jesse Jones did a fine job of that all by his lonesome.) She would pull that *stooopid* string nonstop and that *stooopid* little doll said those *stooopid* things nonstop.

"That outfit looks glorious on you."

"It's a beautiful day to play with your dollie."

"Shall we have some more tea?"

Stooopid, stooopid, stooopid things like that.

So one day when Jesse Jones just couldn't stand it any longer, he took matters into his own hands. His mom had taken Cathy to the mall and left him behind, even though he wanted to go check out the games at the used video game store.

"You're just going to have to learn to be nicer to your sister, Mr. Mean Brother Man," she had said before they walked out.

Jesse Jones hadn't planned on it. He was just walking around the house bored and mad. Then he saw it.

He was more than a little surprised that his sister had forgotten to take it with her. Jesse Jones started by throwing the doll on the floor and stomping on it. And kicking it. Then throwing it against the wall. Over and over again.

"What do you say to that?!" he yelled. "It's a beautiful day to knock the stuffing out of your dumb dollie. Ha, ha, ha!"

He was really having fun now and starting to feel better. Then it happened. Later Jesse Jones didn't really remember exactly how it happened. But the doll's head came off. At first he tried to put it back on, but that didn't work. After that he walked around the house, throwing the head in the air and catching it like a baseball. Eventually, he reached the bathroom.

Later Jesse Jones didn't really remember how the next thing happened either. But somehow or other the doll's head wound up in the toilet. As he was staring at the **disembodied** head just floating there, he heard the front door open.

"Jesse, we're home!"

Jesse Jones thought something like "oh, shoot" and acted quickly. There was only one thing to do.

Even before leaving the bathroom, he heard his sister's screams ripping the house apart.

disembodied: not having a body.

"Noooooooooooooooooooooooooooooo000 OOO!!!" she wailed. "My dollie!" Jesse Jones was born for moments like these. He had to think fast. So he fed his mom some line about Buster being a likely suspect. And to his **astonishment**, his mom bought it.

"I can't believe Buster would do such a thing," his mom said, but there was something in the way she said it that made Jesse Jones feel like she could believe.

His only defense a sad, confused look, Buster did indeed end up taking the fall. He was sentenced to **solitary confinement** in the backyard.

"That, my friend, was a close one," Jesse Jones whispered to himself. "At least that *stooopid* dog is good for something."

When he saw his little sister later that day, her eyes were red and swollen. She was quiet. His teacher would have said she was heartbroken or something sappy like that.

"Serves her right," Jesse Jones thought. It had turned out to be quite an adventure but he had come out all right. More than all right.

Outside, the moon played hide-and-seek behind the oak tree and Buster whined sadly. When his mom said it was bedtime, Jesse Jones didn't argue. He was pooped. Plum tuckered out. He brushed his teeth and went to bed. Then he heard it. Moaning, soft and low.

astonishment: surprise.
solitary confinement: in prison alone, separated from others.

"Why did you do that to me, Jesse? Why?"

The sound was coming from the toilet. It couldn't be coming from the toilet. But it came from the toilet. It came just the same.

"Why, Jesse? Jesse, Why? Whyyyyyy did you tear my head OFF?"

Being Jesse Jones, Jesse Jones got mad. Real mad. And then he got even. He went to the bathroom, flushed the toilet, and smiled. Then he went back to bed. He had no trouble falling asleep. But something woke him in the middle of the night. The voice of the doll was back. It was louder.

"Whyyyyyy, Jesse? WHY?!"

Jesse Jones began to worry that someone might hear, but he was beginning to get scared too. Too scared to go to the bathroom and look to see that there was nothing there. Nothing in the toilet. But what if there were? Better stay in bed, Jesse Jones counseled himself.

"Jesse, what you did to me wasn't RIGHT!" The voice was closer now, and louder and angrier. "And what about poor Cath-EEEEEE?!"

Jesse Jones pulled the covers over his head and for the first time in his life felt real fear. The doll's voice was closer still – it sounded like it was right above his head – and it didn't sound like the doll's voice anymore. It sounded wet and dark and not of this world.

"I-I-I'm sorry," Jesse Jones stuttered and cried.

"It's much too late for that," the voice said. "Now you're coming with MEEEEEEEE!"

The next morning Jesse Jones didn't come down for breakfast. His mother called and called and finally had to go into his room. When she opened the door, the smell almost made her vomit. It was as if the most terrible toilet in the world had backed up and overflowed into the room.

Jesse Jones was never seen again.

Acknowledgements

My thanks to the following: C. B. Colby for writing *Strangely Enough*. It's the book that started me on my way all those years ago. Seymour, *the Master of the Macabre*, for keeping me up way past my bedtime with his terrible movies. John Newland for creating the old *One Step Beyond* TV series. Most episodes weren't that good, but the good ones were bone-chilling. The masterful Alvin Schwartz and Stephen Gammell for the *Scary Stories to Tell in the Dark* series. A very special thanks to the small but ghoulish Penn-Coughin family for its inspiration, contribution, and *inhuman* sacrifice. And my publisher, Wendy Kehoe, for being Wendy Kehoe and everything that that means.

About the Author

In a *previous* life, O. Penn-Coughin was a file clerk, dishwasher, assembler (two hours), casino coin-wrapper (three weeks), delivery guy, and newspaper reporter/editor. Mostly, though, O. Penn-Coughin was an elementary school teacher (almost 20 years). Some of his former students say he was so good it was scary. Others say he was just plain scary.

When not writing or visiting schools, O. Penn-Coughin is out looking for scary stories while hiking, canoeing, snowshoeing, or running. Originally from Argentina, he haunts Bend, Oregon with his wife, two daughters, a sharp-clawed orange cat, and a ghost dog – which still won't fetch.